D1432909

# TENKAI KNIGHTS, GO!

# TENKAI KNIGHTS

展開 騎士

by Brandon T. Snider

Grosset & Dunlap
An Imprint of Penguin Group (USA) LLC

GROSSET & DUNLAP
Published by the Penguin Group
Penguin Group (USA) LLC, 375 Hudson Street, New York, New York 10014, USA

USA | Canada | UK | Ireland | Australia | New Zealand | India | South Africa | China

penguin.com
A Penguin Random House Company

TM Spin Master Ltd. All rights reserved. © 2014 Spin Master Ltd. / Shogaukuken-Shueisia Productions Co., Ltd. All rights reserved. Published by Grosset & Dunlap, a division of Penguin Young Readers Group, 345 Hudson Street, New York, New York 10014. GROSSET & DUNLAP is a trademark of Penguin Group (USA) LLC. Printed in the USA.

ISBN 978-0-448-48349-8                    10 9 8 7 6 5 4 3 2 1

Guren Nash and Ceylan Jones are the Tenkai Knights known as Bravenwolf and Tributon. They had many questions about their powers, so they asked their friend Mr. White if he could help them.

"I have some of the answers you seek," Mr. White said, placing a glowing Brick on the counter. Then a hologram appeared right in front of their eyes!

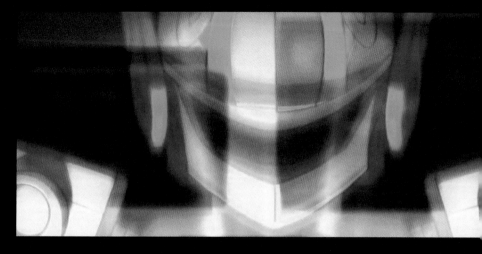

"I am Boreas, Guardian of the Portal," the hologram said. "Many years ago, the Tenkai Knights combined their powers and destroyed the dangerous Tenkai Dragon, scattering its pieces across the galaxy. Now you must find the Dragon Cubes before Vilius destroys the universe."

Guren and Ceylan knew that they were special, but the pressure to save the world was a lot for Ceylan to handle. He had second thoughts about being a hero. "This is too dangerous for me. I give up!" Ceylan explained. "I think I will go grab a milkshake instead."

hat night, Guren dreamed of battling Vilius all by himself. It got him thinking that
be he didn't need Ceylan after all. The next day, the boys went on a school trip
visited a museum where they saw an ancient stone tablet with some very familia
ools on it.

The tablet began to glow, just like the Bricks that the boys carried with them. Suddenly the Tenkai Dragon appeared, and the boys quickly took off to tell Mr. White. He explained that the boys were chosen to be heroes and that their Bricks would remain bonded to them forever.

"I'm no good at being a hero," Ceylan explained. "I didn't ask for this."

"We've been given a big responsibility. It's up to us to do the right thing!" Guren said, shapeshifting himself into Bravenwolf and teleporting to Quarton.

g was happy to see the mighty Bravenwolf return to Quarton for battle!
eeded help retrieving the Dragon Cube from Slyger and Granox, two b
werful warriors. But Bravenwolf really wished that his best friend was th
him.

"Did I miss anything?" a voice called from behind a rock. Ceylan had shapeshifted himself into Tributon and joined Bravenwolf after all! The two friends always had each other's backs. But they had to be careful—danger lurked around every corner.

"Divide and conquer! That is the way of the Corrupted!" commanded Granox.

"I know we weren't invited, but we're crashing this party, too!" said Valorn, a brand-new Tenkai Knight! He and his friend Lydendor appeared out of nowhere to help Bravenwolf and Tributon secure the Dragon Cube and return it to the Corekai for safekeeping.

Bravenwolf and Tributon were thankful that Valorn and Lydendor saved their necks when they needed them. But before they could thank them, the new Tenkai Knights disappeared into thin air. "I wonder if we'll ever see them again," said Tributon.

Later, the boys asked Mr. White if he knew anything about these new Tenkai Knights.

"You must discover the answers on your own. It's part of your training. The truth may be closer than you think!" said Mr. White.

Meanwhile on Quarton, Granox and Slyger told Vilius that all four Tenkai Knights had returned, but they couldn't work together as a team.

"We must get the Dragon Cube back. The time to destroy them is now. Fail me again and I won't be so forgiving!" Vilius said, slamming down his staff in anger.

Back on Earth, Ceylan and Guren followed a pair of suspicious-looking boys into Mr. White's shop. Ceylan noticed that the special portal to Quarton had just been used.

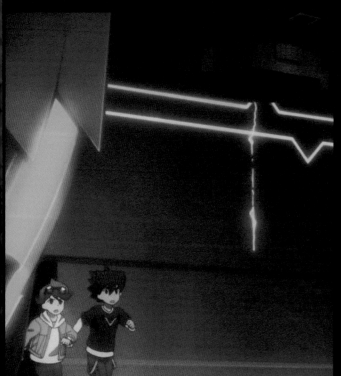

"Okay, mystery knights, we've got you now!" said Ceylan. He and Guren shapeshifted into Tributon and Bravenwolf and followed the trail to Quarton.

On Quarton, Lydendor and Valorn were attacked by an army of vicious Robobeasts as well as Slyger and his Claw of Doom. The heroes hoped to secure the Dragon Cube by themselves, but it would prove very difficult. Thankfully, Bravenwolf and Tributon arrived just in time!

Bravenwolf blasted a Robobeast with Tenkai Energy, and he and Tributon charged in to save Lydendor. The four heroes were outnumbered and decided to return to the Shop of Wonders to figure out their next move.

"We had the bad guys on the ropes till you two showed up!" said the green-haired boy.

"We were only trying to help. I thought we could all work together," said Guren.

Guren and Ceylan wondered why these boys had been given the Tenkai Knights power.

"These guys couldn't fight off a case of the sniffles. We're better off without them!" said Ceylan.

The next day, all four Knights were summoned to the Shop of Wonders by Mr. White.

"The four Tenkai Knights have assembled! Now we can begin," said Mr. White, activating a special message sent from the Guardian Boreas.

"The warlord Vilius was once a Tenkai Knight, but his energy became dark and corrupted. Now he wants to reassemble the Tenkai Dragon so he can take over Quarton and invade Earth. He must be stopped at all costs," said Boreas.

"I guess we'll have to work together after all. Tenkai Knights, go!" said Guren. The four boys quickly powered up and transported to Quarton, where Beag told them how to find the Dragon Cube. In order to save the day, they had to unite as a single force for good!

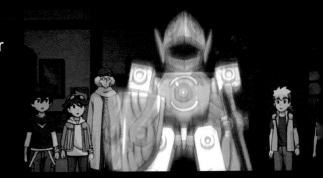

The four heroes blasted into battle, defeating Slyger and his Claw of Doom and securing the Dragon Cube from the evil grip of Vilius. They learned the value of teamwork by sticking together and doing the right thing.

"This teamwork thing isn't so bad. We *are* a team, right?" asked Bravenwolf. Before anyone could answer, the boys transported back to the Shop of Wonders. If they were going to be working together from now on, it was important that they become friends first.

"I'm Chooki," said the blond-haired boy. "And my green-haired friend is Toxsa."

"So it's agreed. We're a team at last!" said Guren. "Welcome to the Tenkai Knights!"